SUSAN ORLEAN

LAZY LITTLE LOAFERS

ILLUSTRATED BY
G. BRIAN KARAS

Abrams Books for Young Readers, New York

The illustrations in this book were made with
gouache, acrylic with pencil, and photo collage.

Library of Congress Cataloging-in-Publication Data:
Orlean, Susan.
Lazy little loafers / by Susan Orlean ; illustrated by G. Brian Karas.
p. cm.
Summary: While walking to school, lugging a heavy backpack through New York City
one morning, a disgruntled child questions why babies are so lazy, spending their days on
useless activities such as napping and babbling rather than getting jobs.
ISBN 978-0-8109-7027-4
[1. Babies—Fiction. 2. New York (N.Y.)—Fiction. 3. Humorous stories.]
I. Karas, G. Brian, ill. II. Title.

PZ7.O6328Shi 2008
[E]—dc22
2007042047

Book design by Chad W. Beckerman

Published in 2008 by Abrams Books for Young Readers,
an imprint of Harry N. Abrams, Inc.

Printed and bound in U.S.A.
10 9 8 7 6 5 4 3 2 1

HNA
harry n. abrams, inc.
a subsidiary of La Martinière Groupe

115 West 18th Street
New York, NY 10011
www.hnabooks.com

For Austin, my very own
lazy little loafer, with love
—S.O.

For Trudy, with love
—G.B.K.

Here's a question for you: Why don't more babies work?

Excuse me, did I say "more"? I mean, why don't any babies work? After all, there are millions of babies around, and most of them, in my opinion, seem to spend their days doing nothing much at all.

There are so many jobs in the world—
but babies never do any of them!
Why aren't babies working? I have been
trying to figure it out.

One recent autumn morning, I loaded up my backpack and headed for school. A baby was right behind me. *Aha!* I thought. *A perfect opportunity to study a typical example of the breed.* He was lounging in his stroller, waving his bottle and clutching a teddy bear—you know what they're like.

I took a good look at him lying there and knew at least part
of the answer: You don't have to be a genius to realize that
babies are just lazy.

And think of that same baby, same lazy pose, but imagine him wearing dark sunglasses—you see it all the time. Supposedly, it has to do with UV rays, but have you ever noticed that a baby with sunglasses looks not just lazy, but lazy and snobby?! Like a lazy, snobby movie star who can't be bothered to give you an autograph—even if he knew how to write.

the ONE and ONLY BABY!
"Thrilling !!" "A BLAST !!"

Some of these babies wearing sunglasses might actually be working in show business—a few of them, anyway. But there probably aren't that many roles for chubby little people. And everyone knows that babies change really fast—sometimes the cutest ones aren't so cute in a matter of weeks. Plus, they can't even read a script!

And as far as model superbabies go, I'm not sure they're real—after all, you can do just about anything with digital photography.

The one job that babies seem willing and eager to do is stroller pushing. Well, big deal, since (a) they're actually very bad at it, and (b) am I the only one who doesn't think that pushing a stroller is a reason to celebrate? Not compared to the things *real* kids have to do, like making our own beds and doing homework!

Elevator button pushing? Sure, every baby does it, but it's not a job; it's a prank. (Unless you really need to stop on every floor, which is NEVER.)

And have you watched babies trying to walk? Is it possible they don't work but still go out for a three-bottle lunch and get a little tipsy?

Of course, babies do a lot of unpaid research on stand-up (and fall-down) comedy and how to express yourself by babbling nothing but "Goo goo, gaa gaa" all day long—but I happen to know that "research" is just another way of saying that Someone Else Pays for My Pampers.

Anyway, on this particular day, while I was conducting my study, I crossed through Central Park on the way to school. As usual, the park was filled with babies, all loafing around and looking as happy as clams.

Of course babies love warm fall days—and what's not to like? While the rest of us are hard at work taking tests, giving book reports, and figuring out tough math questions, the babies hang out in the park, relaxed and cheerful— and mostly naked. Unlike us big kids, they don't have to wear back-to-school clothes and stiff new shoes and carry tons of books on their shoulders!

So what exactly were these lazy little loafers doing on this warm morning?

Oh, a lot of important stuff: They were snacking and waving at all the dogs passing by and hanging out with their friends—in other words, they were doing everything I might do on a nice September day if I didn't have to go to school.

The baby who had been following me was looking especially relaxed and cheerful, so I decided to stop and talk to him, and suggest that he start thinking about getting a job since it looked like he had a lot of spare time.

But as I got close, he turned his attention to one of his toes and to the blade of grass in his fist.

I know that look: I use it in the school cafeteria when I don't feel like having someone sit next to me. It always works for me, and it worked like a charm for the baby.

I could tell he wasn't going to listen to me—
he was settling in for a nice long, lazy day with his
companion. So I shrugged and headed to school.

Just as I arrived, I figured out the answer to my question. You want to know the reason babies don't work?

They're too smart.